Rainbow Edition

The FRIENDS of JIMMY

The FRIENDS of JIMMY

Written and Illustrated by

GERTRUDE ALICE KAY

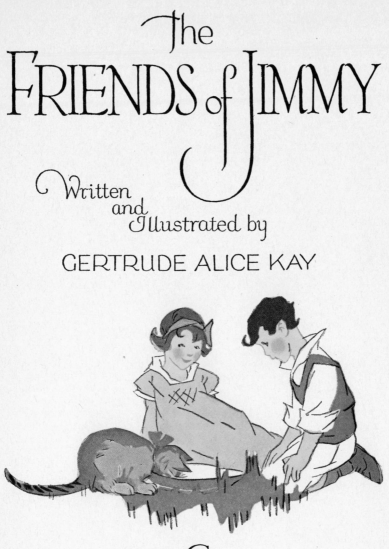

Published by
THE WISE-PARSLOW COMPANY
NEW YORK

R0116747328

jFICK1796fr

To
girls and boys everywhere
who seek adventure and find
it in their own neighborhood.

HOW would you like to live in a funny little old building upstairs, over the cobbler's shop, like Jimmy, and have your Mother, a dressmaker, who made dresses for ladies who were all the time ringing the doorbell? I must tell you they were all very nice ladies and sometimes gave him a penny or so, but once one of them gave him a little green sprinkling can to water the geraniums in the flower boxes.

Well this Jimmy, the story is about, lived in the funny little old building, upstairs, over the cobbler's shop, and his Mother was the dressmaker and had big scissors to cut with, and pink paper patterns and billions of needles and pins and a tape measure that unwound. And whenever the doorbell rang Jimmy almost fell all the way down stairs in his haste to see which one of the nice ladies was there.

Now the reason one of the ladies brought him the green sprinkling can was she saw Jimmy watering the geraniums in the window boxes with his mother's teapot, which of course wasn't the thing to do at all. She said, "My, my!" And the next time she came she brought a sprinkling can. She held the pretty shining green thing out to Jimmy to take and keep for his. He was delighted. So the plants were watered many times each day and soon got *very* tall and almost stopped having flowers. Jimmy's mother said that perhaps that was the reason.

Nice as it was living upstairs, over the cobbler's shop and having lots of rings at the doorbell and a green sprinkling can, what was even nicer, was having friends all up and down the street—most especially across the street at the boarding house. Now this boarding house was both wide and tall, and had a porch with vines and lots of windows and belonged to the Boarding House Ladies, who were sisters. One was thin and the other was not. They liked Jimmy very much and he liked *them* very much. In their kitchen he was allowed to eat as many raisins as he could hold, to scrape the cake dough out of the big yellow bowl— and the first and hottest cookie out of the oven was *his*.

But of all the nice people in the house the Funny Man was Jimmy's best friend. You see the Funny Man was not at all like other grown-up persons for you could have jokes with him. That is, you could have jokes *together*, and you always knew for sure that he was not laughing at you. He could play pretend games, or draw pictures of anything at all, or tell stories, without first making you promise to be good, or to go to bed early, or stop eating with your fingers. He didn't care very much about things like that.

Most everybody in the boarding house worked, all but the Funny Man and several old ladies who only made tatting. But he went downtown most every day after letters out of the postoffice or to the bank, where he kept his money. So you see he was never so busy that he would have to say, 'Now Jimmy *please* be quiet,' or 'Now Jimmy *please* run along for a while.' Not like Jimmie's busy Mother sometimes did, or the Boarding House Ladies.

And the Funny Man even liked to answer questions. If you asked Jimmy what he was like he would probably say, "He's little, not much bigger than I. He wears glasses and his face crinkles because he laughs so much." You can easily see he wasn't like other grown up persons, who read newspapers all the time, and have headaches and rheumatism, and scold about politics and the weather and business. And you never wondered what to do and what to talk about when you were with him, because he always *knew*. So the Funny Man was about Jimmie's best friend—except his mother. But Mothers of course are different from anybody else and then Jimmie's was always so busy making dresses, so that she could pay the cobbler for letting them live upstairs, and the grocery man for the potatoes and things that they ate for dinner.

Another of Jimmie's friends was the Popcorn Man who had a goat, named Bill, who sometimes stood up on his hind legs when he was told. Jimmy liked the Popcorn Man because he often allowed him to watch the corn popper when he went around the corner after something. And the goat was friendly too—always looked as if he was about to laugh at something.

Then of course there was Banana John—the Funny Man named him that. He kept the fruit store and had a parrot. Banana John was much nicer than his parrot.

Several of the old ladies who lived at the boarding house were Jimmie's friends too. They were always patching quilts and when *they* told a story it always started—'Once upon a time when I was a little girl'—stories not at all like the Funny Man's. But they were always good to him and often tied up a hurt finger or gave him throat lozenges which are a sort of candy. Several of them had cross little dogs that growled even if you *didn't* nudge them with your foot. The Funny Man said that the dogs weren't any good because they never buried bones, or got into fights. Sometimes the old ladies put on their bonnets and shawls and took the dogs out walking. But never down where the Popcorn Man's goat was. No *indeed*.

Now if you went *down* the street there were stores, every kind, and the post office and the bank. Then if you went

the other way, *up* the street, there was the church and lots
of houses. Another friend of Jimmie's, the Scratch Cat and
her sister, the Politest Child, lived in the big yellow house
with green shutters and a white fence. And they had a
baby carriage and a live baby who rode in it. It was their
brother and Ellen was the nurse. And of course they had
a mother and father too.

It was Ellen who first gave the Scratch Cat that name,
though it wasn't like her unless she was very, *very* naughty.

Which she wasn't often. You had to like her because she always gave you the biggest half of things and then she had such pretty red curls.

Jimmy thought that the Politest Child was nice too but she always cried if she got grass stain on her apron. Grown-up persons thought her quite remarkable.

So you see that Jimmy had lots of friends up and down the street—in the stores and in the houses too. In the stores they said he was "bright as a dollar." And the ladies in the houses always said "such a good little boy because he wipes his mother's dishes and runs errands."

Then there was the Grocery Boy and Jeff. The Grocery Boy drove a delivery wagon and took baskets of potatoes and canned peaches and such things to people's back doors.

But Jeff was the livery stable boy and hitched and un-hitched horses and polished carriages. Sometimes he took Jimmy on rides and drove like lightning. He was one of Jimmie's *best* friends.

And now you will hear more about these friends of Jimmy and the good times he was always having with them.

*　　*　　*　　*　　*

About the first thing that Jimmy did every morning—even before he got dressed, was to fill the little green sprinkling can and water the flower boxes. Then maybe at noon when he had his dinner he'd water them again, because of course they'd be thirsty. And the same at supper time. Then one day the Funny Man over on the porch at the boarding house, said "Hey, hey, Jimmy why not water the telegraph pole too and see what happens."

Now what do you suppose he meant by that? Well Jimmy didn't know either. You see the telegraph pole was just exactly outside Jimmie's window and was always there winter and summer. So Jimmy went skipping across the street.

The Funny Man had his own chair in one corner of the

porch, and because his legs weren't very long he hooked them back underneath.

"What did telegraph poles used to be?" asked Jimmy.

"Tall, straight trees, with branches, and leaves and birds' nests," answered the Funny Man.

Jimmy had never thought about that before. Poor old skinny telegraph poles—no branches, no leaves, no birds' nests, having to stand still in rows through the towns and along the country roads—winter and summer, and just hold up wires.

"Well, what are the wires for?" was Jimmie's next question.

"To carry telegraph messages," answered the Funny Man. Then he knew those words were too big, so he said, "To carry stories back and forth between folks." Of course that isn't exactly what happens, but it's near enough.

You can see for yourself that Jimmy couldn't understand this at all. Folks sending stories back and forth over wires strung on tall poles. He couldn't even straighten out the questions inside of his own head, so that he could ask them.

"I tell you what I'll do," said the Funny Man. "I'll catch a story for you some day, if you'll water the poor old telegraph pole once in a while instead of your window boxes."

Jimmy said he would. "But how do you catch the stories?"

"Well," said the Funny Man. "Everybody can't do it I suppose. They drop off mostly at night long after you are asleep. So when I think that it's about time for one, I go out and hold my hat under the wires. Then when the hat begins to feel heavy I put it back on my head and go home. The next morning I can tell by the way my head feels that there is a story in it. Queer isn't it? So that very day I tell it to you so I won't forget it. And that's all there is to it—catching the story in your hat, then putting the hat on your head. And the first thing you know the story is inside your head—just like that!"

"But why should I water the telegraph pole?" asked Jimmy. "Would it like me to water it?"

"Yes, I am sure it would," said the Funny Man. "For you see nobody pays any attention to telegraph poles except to hitch their horses to them, and that wouldn't make you feel so very good since horses usually chew whatever they are hitched to. You see if you had once been a fine big tree with thousands of leaves to swish in the wind and long branches to wave around in the sky, you'd feel very sad to have them all stripped off and be made to stand on a pavement where people pass back and forth all day long without ever once saying, 'My what a fine tall tree that is.' The way they once did."

"That's so," said Jimmy on the top step.

"Yes, I think it is," said the Funny Man in the corner.

"Well what will some of the stories be about?" asked Jimmy.

"What would you like them to be about?" asked the Funny Man.

"About Christmas," said Jimmy.

"Not Christmas now *surely*," said the Funny Man. "This is summer. Pick on something else."

"About a monkey," said Jimmy.

"And what else?" asked the Funny Man.

"A witch," said Jimmy.

"And what else?" asked the Funny Man.

"Oh," said Jimmy, "lots and *lots* of things. Princes and giants and goblins and sea monsters. And Santa Claus of course."

"That's a lot of things," said the Funny Man, "we'll see."

Just then Jimmie's mother put her head out of the window and called to him that she wanted him to go to the dry goods store on an errand. *Right away*.

"Well goodbye," said Jimmy.

"Come back again," said the Funny Man.

One spool of white number sixty, one paper of pins, one card of hooks and eyes and a yard and a quarter "like sample," was what Jimmie's mother wanted. She pinned the sample on the front of his coat. He was used to going on errands to the dry-goods store and never forgot, or made mistakes, but that was because he kept saying them over and over to himself all the way. Supposing now if he had stopped to talk to the Popcorn Man, or to pat Bill, the goat, who was laughing and jumping around—why, of course he would have forgotten the very thing that she needed most. Instead he zigzagged across to the other side of the street and hurried on. Then suddenly back again for he was coming to the fruit stand where the parrot was. Sometimes it was hard to pass by there in a hurry for there were all those rows of peaches and pears to look at—and the Fruit Store Man often gave Jimmy the ones that had soft places in them. And if the parrot wasn't too cross he'd say, "hello."

When Jimmy reached the dry-goods store he was still whispering "One spool of sixty white, one paper of pins," and so on. He told them to Miss Mazie, who always stood behind the counter by the window. She tied the things up in a paper, wrote it in her book and told Jimmy to take them *straight* home to his mother. Just as if he wouldn't.

But as Jimmy came out of the dry-goods store there stood the Scratch Cat, her sister, the Politest Child, and Ellen who was pushing the baby carriage.

"Hello," said Jimmy.

"Where are you going?" said the Scratch Cat, instead of saying hello back.

"Home," said Jimmy, pushing the package higher under his arm.

"Oh, come on with us," said the Scratch Cat, and her eyes glittered as if she knew something surprising.

"Where?" asked Jimmy.

"To see a big, *big* fish," she answered.

"You are not *sure*," said Ellen.

"Yes, I am," said the Scratch Cat. "The Grocery Boy told me all about it. It's as big as a house and is a sea monster."

So off they went, baby and all, down the street toward the place where you could see the tip-tops of the ships sticking up in the sky. Jimmy wasn't allowed to go down there by himself but the Funny Man took him once a long time ago, so he knew what a fine place it was. There were all sorts of things piled up, boxes and barrels, with ropes everywhere and big boats and little boats. It was *wonderful*.

The Scratch Cat, who was jumping a rope, instead of walking, managed to tell Jimmy that the Grocery Boy had told Ellen that a big, *big* fish—a whale maybe, was tied to the dock and weighed as much as a house, and that everybody was going to see it. And sure enough they met lots of men and boys coming back, who *had* seen it. But they were all talking about "ten cents a look." Whatever that meant.

So after a while they reached the dock where the big fish was supposed to be. It took them such a long time because the Politest Child insisted on stopping and pushing her nose against all the shop windows and looking over all the garden fences. She wasn't at all interested in seeing the big fish for she knew that it wouldn't smell good. And now even Ellen was beginning to think that maybe they shouldn't be there. Then she spied a big sign painted in white paint on the sidewalk. And it said:

See the Big Sea Monster
for
10c a look.

"That settles it, who would pay 10c to look at any fish that ever swam," said Ellen.

"Oh, please, kind Ellen, let us go just a tiny little bit nearer," teased the Scratch Cat. Ellen didn't want to, but the Scratch Cat begged so hard that they went on, though the Politest Child hung back and complained about how everything smelled.

But when they got there, there was a big thick rope tied across and men and boys were standing so close that even if you had paid 10c for a look most likely you couldn't have seen anything. The Scratch Cat started to squirm and push and use her elbows and heels—till Ellen grabbed her back.

So there seemed to be nothing to do but turn around and go home. *Now* the Politest Child was the gayest and skipped ahead of everyone for she never wanted to see a sea monster. But Jimmy and the Scratch Cat were disappointed. They were wondering what it looked like.

Then they saw the Popcorn wagon and Ellen, who was kind, bought them a bag for five cents. But it was soon gone.

After that they watched Bill do his tricks, which were two in number, and which they had seen many times before. One was to stand up straight on his back legs, the other was to get down on his knees in front.

The next place they stopped was the fruit store where they said 'hello' a lot of times to the parrot. But the parrot was sulky and crowded in back of the bananas and wouldn't come out.

Then all of a sudden Jimmy saw Miss Mazie the dry goods lady with her hat tipped over her nose, going home to dinner. And that made him remember how sharply she had looked at him when she told him to take the bundle *straight* home to his mother. It made him feel queer inside—scared and ashamed, for now he remembered that his mother had said 'to hurry back for she needed the sixty white right away.' Then who should he see but the Funny Man hurrying down the street and looking every which way at once. When he spied Jimmy he stood still and looked as if he had a big notion to be cross. But all he said was, "Well, Young Man." And behind him came Jimmie's mother and the

Boarding House Ladies. His mother said, "What does this mean?" And the Boarding House Ladies said, "How you scared us Jimmy, we thought that you were lost."

The Scratch Cat seemed willing to do the talking, so Jimmy kept quiet and let her tell all about it, how they went down to see the sea monster, but that it cost 10c to look at it, and Ellen had only five. So they had popcorn instead.

Then they all turned around and nobody was scared about anything any longer. Jimmie's mother walked beside him, and she told him that she really *must* punish him—though she didn't know just how. So Jimmy looked very sad for Jimmy. And the Funny Man pinched his ear just to show that they were still friends.

That evening Jimmy had to go to bed early—*before* dark. His mother was sure that it would make him remember never, *never* to run away again. And as he stood in the front window looking over toward the Boarding House, the Funny Man called, "Maybe I'll catch a telegram story tonight."

"Really truly?" asked Jimmy.

"I'll try," said the Funny Man.

"What will it be about?" asked Jimmy.

"How would a Sea Monster story do?" asked the Funny Man.

Jimmy clapped his hands. "I'll come over *early*," he called back.

Then his mother said that he must go to bed at once, so he yelled "Goodnight," across the street and climbed into bed.

Now Jimmy thought he'd like to stay awake and peep and maybe see the Funny Man hold his hat and catch the telegram story when it dropped off the wires. But instead of that he went to sleep.

"What's today?" said Jimmy next morning to his mother.

"Well, its raining to start with," she said. "And a good day for a little fellow to help his mother wipe dishes and pick up the stray pins and needles on the sewing room floor. And then maybe fold up all the paper patterns and put them away in the pattern box."

"And then?" asked Jimmy.

"Well what then?" asked his mother.

"Go over to see the Funny Man?"

"Most likely," answered his mother.

So Jimmy jumped into his clothes like a flash and as soon as breakfast and the dishes were over he began to pick up pins and needles. They were everywhere. When that was done he folded the pink paper patterns and laid them in the pattern box.

"And now Mother?" he said.

"All finished?" asked his mother.

"Every bit."

Jimmy got across the street in such a hurry the rain didn't have a chance to fall on him. On such days he never looked for the Funny Man on the porch, but upstairs in his room. It was such a nice rainy day room. The ceiling came slanting down to the windows, and if you sat with your back against the wall it was warm where the kitchen chimney came up. And there were no end of interesting things all about and you could pick them up and ask questions about them too. The Funny Man didn't care.

When Jimmy reached the top of the stairs he saw that the Funny Man's door stood open a little bit, so he poked his head in.

"Did you get it?" he asked.

"Get what?" said the Funny Man, pretending.

"You know," said Jimmy. "The Sea Monster story, of course."

"Well," said the Funny Man, "Here's what dropped off the wires." And he unfolded a yellow paper.

Jimmy scrambled up on his lap and looked.

"Read it," he said. So the Funny Man put on his glasses and read:

To

    Felix the Fierce
    Castle of Shakeafist
    Mount Thunder Clap

    Prince swam away with Sea Monster and twin mermaids.

                  Herman the Huge
                  Castle Squirmandskip
                  By the Sea

"Well what does that mean?" asked Jimmy.

"I'll explain," said the Funny Man. So here's the story word for word just as he told it to Jimmy.

Now everybody who lived in a certain neighborhood—a long, long way from here, had heard of the giants, Felix the Fierce and Herman the Huge, who were just what you might expect them to be or even more so. Regular rascals they were and giants besides. And living miserably between the castles of these two giants was the Peaceable Prince. Not a giant of course and just what you might imagine from *his* name—peace loving, easy going and amiable—but *unlucky*. In fact I doubt if anyone ever lived who was quite so unlucky. You see the lightning always struck *his* chimney. The wind always lifted off *his* roof and *his* horse always went lame, even though his neighbors went along, year in and year out without any of these things happening to them. It was the strangest thing. And it was almost funny because the Peaceable Prince was the accepted suitor of the Princess of *Luck Hill*.

Now Luck Hill wasn't anywhere round-about but miles and miles away. It was said to be one of the wonders of the world, for nothing ever went wrong there. The weather always exactly suited everyone. The crops never failed. Everyone was rich and healthy. All the women were beautiful and all the men were honest, not to mention brave.

And if you'll believe it the Peaceable Prince couldn't manage by hook or crook to get there. Why not? Because Felix who lived on a mountain top where he could see half of everything that happened, and Herman who lived by the sea and could see the other half, wouldn't let him. And why not? Just because they didn't like him. The Peaceable Prince was too amiable. He annoyed them into fits of rage, because he never lost his temper and never ranted and roared as they did. It delighted them to pester him. So they made his life a bad dream.

Just as his garden looked most promising they'd come riding with their horsemen, and after they were gone, no one would ever guess there had been a garden. Then when the fruit was beginning to ripen on the trees, the ruffians would shake them bare.

But to all that, the Peaceable Prince would only say, "It's too early in the day to lose one's temper," or else "It's now too late, according to the clock." And then he'd sing or whistle to himself and finally forget all about it, which of course, made the giants feel foolish. You see the Peaceable Prince was *sure* that sometime, sooner or later, everything would come right. That probably the wind would never take his roof away again, that his horse would get over his lameness, some day the giants would become friendly neighbors and that the lovely Princess of Luck Hill would wait for him. So he whistled and sang.

Now strangely enough The Peaceable Prince had for a housekeeper an old woman named Dora Dirge and like the other people in this story she was just like her name. Her chief delight was to look ahead and worry about the things that *might* happen in years to come. True she found plenty of real worries in the household of the unlucky Prince, so whenever the latch clicked she came scampering to meet him to say that the chimney smoked or the drain was clogged or some other thing gone wrong. And while he ate his poor meal, she would stand by to assure him that he grew poorer and poorer with every passing day. And just what did he plan to do when the last penny was gone,

and with only a leaky roof overhead and all the windows broken? Such a dreary woman. She spoiled his appetite. So the Peaceable Prince was really getting thin. And you know you don't feel quite so much like whistling and singing when you are losing weight.

So sometimes to get away from all this he used to go down to sit in the sand by a little corner of the sea which was hidden from the view of Felix and Herman, but best of all out of the reach of Dora Dirge's mournful voice.

So one day while he sat there thinking things over and trying to make himself believe that they were not quite as bad as they seemed, suddenly two heads, exactly alike, appeared, sticking straight up out of the sea.

"Why good morning, little sisters—and twins too, if I may say so."

"Twin sisters, and mermaids as well," answered the heads.

"Twin-sister-mermaids—a very pretty idea," said the Prince.

"Thanks very much," said the mermaids.

Then there was a pause in the conversation for as you know mermaids, like fish, are shy. And the Prince was rather shy too, probably because he realized what a shabby fellow he looked.

So, just to start things, one of the mermaids asked about the crops, as she had sometimes heard real people do.

But the Prince only shrugged his shoulders.

Then the other mermaid, just to help things along, asked if he had nice neighbors.

At that the Prince laughed. Then he told them that Felix the Fierce lived on one side of him and Herman the Huge on the other.

"Oh dear, oh dear!" sighed the twin mermaids, spreading their long fingers and rolling their round eyes. You see everybody knew what rascals the Giants were.

"Why not swim away?" whispered one mermaid.

"Why not, indeed?" whispered the other.

"I'm not a good swimmer," confessed the Prince.

"We'll help you," said the Sisters.

"Good girls," said the Prince, "Mermaids I mean, but where would we go?"

"Any where—in the water," answered the Mermaids.

"But I want to go to a hill—*Luck Hill* to be accurate, and one does not swim to get there. He needs a horse, and mine of course, has gone lame. But even so, either Felix or Herman would see us and that would end everything."

Now that was different. The Twin-Sister Mermaids looked puzzled.

"Let's ask the Monster," they said.

"Oh, please don't do that," said the Prince nervously. "A giant is bad enough. A monster would be *much* too much."

But they assured him that this Monster wasn't the same thing at all. He was a Sea Monster, which is really only an over-sized fish.

"That makes quite a lot of difference," agreed the Prince. So the Mermaids sank out of sight beneath the surface of the sea to talk things over with their friend. Presently the twin heads came in sight once more.

"Everything is arranged," said they.

"When do we leave?" asked the Prince.

"Any time," they answered. And just then a whirlpool began to whirl and the Sea Monster himself appeared in the middle of it. But after knowing Felix and Herman the Prince thought the Sea Monster a very mild looking fish. True he had a big mouth, but other parts of him glistened and he had a splendid swishing tail and fins.

The Prince wasn't in the least bit nervous, and said, "Good morning."

The Sea Monster only flashed his tail in reply. "He does not speak the same language," explained the Sisters.

"But he understands everything." It seems that he knew all about Luck Hill and the lovely Princess who lived in the castle that perched on the top of it—the Princess who was forlornly waiting for the suitor who failed to claim her. And had the Prince ever heard of her?

He said that he had. In fact he was himself that very Prince.

This delighted the Twin-Sister Mermaids who were romantic. They clapped their hands.

"Let's start at once," they said.

But the Prince felt that he should really run back and say good bye to Dora Dirge, before starting. He meant to tell her that she could have all his old worries. Felix and Herman, leaky roof, smoky chimney, broken windows, lame horse—everything. All hers. Dora Dirge came near being pleased. But as he crossed the threshold for the last time, she told him in a mournful voice that she expected to hear soon that he was drowned or devoured—or disappointed with the Princess. Probably all three. And she started wringing her hands over what might happen.

Then the Prince, seated on the Sea Monster's back, with a mermaid splashing along on each side of him, set off just at sun-set. All went well till they came to the Castle of Squirmandskip by the Sea. There standing on the shore was Herman the Huge, scowling and grim with arms folded across his immense chest.

"Dive," screamed the mermaids, disappearing from sight. And of course the Sea Monster dived too, carrying the Prince along with him, down, down into a terrible whirlpool. Then he was sure that he was lost as Dora Dirge had said—by drowning. But no,—for suddenly he found himself warm and snug inside the Sea Monster's big mouth.

"I'm to be devoured then," said the Prince to himself. But nothing of the sort happened and when they were safely passed Herman's view they all came up to the top, none the worse. However, Herman had seen them and was in a terrible rage and rushed off and sent the telegram which dropped off the wires into my hat and which I have read to you.

So, of course, Felix the Fierce never received it and they got safely away and finally reached a beautiful beach with Luck Hill rising splendidly above it.

And the lovely Princess who had watched constantly from her tower saw them coming and came running down to meet them.

Again Dora Dirge was mistaken. Nobody could have

found fault, for she was all a beautiful Princess should be—
blue eyes, golden hair and pink cheeks.

Everything came about just as the Peaceable Prince always told himself it would. Even the giants, though he
never saw them again, finally settled down to being well
behaved giants. And the wedding of the Prince and Princess was on the beach and the Mermaids were the bride's
attendants and the Sea Monster gave them his blessing,
along with a great amount of treasure which he obligingly
brought up from the bottom of the ocean. So like every
Prince and Princess they lived happily ever after.

"Do you suppose that it's the same Sea Monster as the
one down here?" asked Jimmy.

"No telling," said the Funny Man.

However, when the Grocery Boy came, he said that the
big fish had got away or something. So they never knew.
But it *might* have been.

Something nice and surprising happened to Jimmy. He had a dollar in his pocket. This is the way it came about. One day when he was running across the street to see the Funny Man he saw some spectacles right in the middle of the road. Of course he picked them up *quickly* before anything could happen to them, and took them over to show to the Funny Man. And he said, "Well, well, somebody will be glad to get *those* back. Like as not they'll give you a reward."

Now maybe you don't know what a reward is. Jimmy didn't either. It means they are so glad to get back whatever they lost that they say "Here's a dollar, take it and get yourself something nice." Well that's what happened to Jimmy. It seems the drug store man had lost his spectacles and didn't know what in the world to do without them, for he couldn't read or mix medicine or anything. So when he heard that a little boy, up the street, had found them, and they weren't stepped on or bent, he said, "Send him in with them and I'll give him a reward." So Jimmy hurried down with the spectacles and the drug store man handed him a dollar, and told him not to lose it.

Now maybe you aren't big enough yet to have a dollar of your own, but when you do get your first one you'll never forget how it feels. Jimmie's mother thought that he ought to put it in his bank where he had a few pennies ladies had given him. But Jimmy had two pockets, one on each side, and he wanted to carry his money around with him the way big fellows do. So his mother sewed it in and told him not to lose it or spend it foolishly. Of course Jimmy said that he wouldn't, and was very proud indeed. He loved to slip his hand in and make sure that it was there.

Then one day after he had picked up all the needles and pins and watered the window boxes, he found that he hadn't anything much to do. The Funny Man had gone down town to attend to things and Jimmy felt lonesome.

"I wish that I had a pet to play with," he said, "A puppy or a kitten. Wouldn't that be nice, Mother?"

"Well not up here, Jimmy dear," said his Mother. "People who live in such little places as this can't have puppies and kittens about. The poor little things might get stepped on."

Just then the stair door banged open, and the Scratch Cat called, "Jimmy, Jimmy come and go on an errand with me."

"I'm coming," yelled Jimmy.

The Politest Child was taking a music lesson. So Jimmy and the Scratch Cat decided to go through the alley. You see the Politest Child didn't like the alley. But it really was a fine place. You could go that way and get to the stores just the same, and it was a lot more interesting than the street. In the first place the livery stable was there and Jeff, the stable boy, was friendly and always allowed them to climb up into the empty buggies and crack the whip just as if a real horse was hitched up.

But today when he saw them coming he told them he had a present for each of them. And you know how that makes you feel! Well, what do you suppose the presents were? Kittens—just like little soft balls, all curled up fast asleep—in a basket. And there sat the old mother blinking and didn't seem to care a bit if Jeff gave them all away.

"You can have your choice," said Jeff, holding up gray ones, black and white, and then yellow, so they could see them all.

Jimmy liked the black and white one. The Scratch Cat chose the yellow kitten.

Then poor Jimmy remembered what his Mother had said that very day about having a pet and so he put the kitten back into the basket, with its mother, and said that he wasn't *allowed*. Of course you know how that makes you feel after someone has given you something.

Then the Scratch Cat, who felt sorry for him, told him

that she'd keep the yellow one, and that they'd own it together and that it could eat and sleep at her house. But that they'd both boss it. You see she was very generous. So they both said "Thank you" to Jeff and went on down the alley toward the street, for the Scratch Cat had to do her errand.

They looked in everywhere as they went along and when they came to the queer, queer little house where the old woman lived who had a goose, they stopped. One day the Funny Man had called her Old Mother Goose, so Jimmy wondered if she ever had *really* ridden on it. It was a big goose though, with such a tall neck, and it snapped at you with its bill, if you went inside the fence, and quacked and hissed.

Now the old woman, poor as she was, fed it a great deal because she was getting it ready to sell. She asked everybody who passed in the alley if they didn't want to buy a fine, fat goose. But nobody needed a goose **right** then, and it got bigger and bigger every day.

Now the old woman must have been very poor indeed for places where the windows were broken were stuffed with rags and papers, and Jimmy thought that her kitchen looked as if there *never* was anything to eat in it. Not even scraps, for the goose ate them all.

Well, today as the children came along the alley, both patting the yellow kitten at once, though Jimmy was holding it, they saw something that looked really very funny. It was the goose looking over the fence, just like a horse or a cow. You see it had grown so tall that its head was hanging over.

"Let's feed it something," said Jimmy, so he pulled some grass and held it near. And though the goose had friendly eyes, the yellow kitten was so scared that it dug its claws into Jimmy. Just then the old woman came out and asked in a shaky voice if they knew anyone that wanted to buy a nice fat goose.

"How much does it cost?" asked Jimmy, just like a grown-up person.

Then the old woman looked pretty sad and said that she guessed that she'd let him have it for a dollar. But you know Jimmy didn't really mean to *buy* the goose, but only to ask how much it was. Probably nobody had ever asked even *that* before, so that was why the old woman thought that he wanted to buy it.

The next thing that they knew she opened the gate and told them to take the goose. So Jimmy put his hand in his pocket and pulled out the stitches that held the dollar safe. He felt funny too. The old woman said that he could lead the goose by a string, which she fastened to its short yellow leg. Then Jimmy handed her the dollar.

Things had happened before he had time to think about them, as all grown-ups know they often do.

"My," said the Scratch Cat, in a sort of whisper, "now you've spent your dollar." But she thought it very wonderful too for Jimmy acted just like men do.

"It's to be my pet," said Jimmy, "and maybe I can ride on its back and teach it fancy tricks."

Then the old woman opened the gate and they started down the alley. The goose walked very slowly, looking this way and that, as probably it had never been out much before. Jimmy felt very proud as people stopped and looked and somebody asked where he was taking it, and he said home, he guessed. Then for the first time he wondered just *what* his mother would say and where the goose would sleep.

But on they went and everything seemed to be all right till they turned into the street where there were people and wagons making a lot of noise. Then suddenly the goose seemed to change. It spread out its big white wings and stretched out its neck in front making dangerous noises. So Jimmy and the Scratch Cat kept behind it for it was snapping with its bill and hissing.

"Now, what shall I do?" asked Jimmy in a shaky voice.

"I don't know," said the Scratch Cat, "unless you let it go."

"But it cost a dollar," answered Jimmy, ready to cry. My! but they were both scared, the kitten, too.

And you never saw a goose act the way that one did. Even big ladies were scared and got inside of doorways. Then the worst thing happened. The goose turned around

all of a sudden and looked as if it were going to eat Jimmy
and the Scratch Cat and the kitten all in one mouthful.
My, how they did run! The next thing, all the men and
boys were chasing the goose and there was yelling and
quacking up and down the street. Finally a big boy caught
it and held its wings down tight.

"Who owns this goose?" he yelled.

"I do," said Jimmy.

Why all the folks in the doorways laughed he didn't know.
And there stood the Funny Man, too, laughing with everyone else.

"Where did *you* get it?" he asked.

"Paid a dollar for it," said Jimmy proudly.

"Don't you want to sell it to me?" asked the Funny
Man.

"Yes," said Jimmy, feeling in his pocket where the
dollar had been.

So that's about all, except that the Funny Man told
the big boy who caught the goose to take it around to the
back door of the boarding house. Then he gave Jimmy
another dollar and told him to come over to dinner tomorrow, and bring his mother—because it was Sunday and
they might have a roast goose.

The next day after they had had roast goose at the boarding house was Monday, and Jimmy and the Scratch Cat were sitting on the steps talking to the Funny Man.

They had been talking about Jimmie's dollar and how tightly his mother had sewed it in this time so that he wouldn't buy geese or anything. Now Jimmie had been thinking that he'd like to have some of the other kind of money too—nickels and dimes that rattled when you ran. The Scratch Cat thought so too.

"How do people get money?" asked Jimmy.

"Different ways," said the Funny Man. "Some earn it, some make it and others have it given to them. Sometimes they find it, too, but if they are honest they give it back. The best way to get it is to earn it."

"Well then, let's earn some," said the Scratch Cat, looking firm.

"How?" asked Jimmy, remembering that you have to really do something like finding spectacles or working before you get paid.

But the Scratch Cat had nothing to say because she couldn't think of a thing that they might do.

"Well," said Jimmy, "we might go errands for people."

"That wouldn't do," said the Funny Man, "for like as not you'd forget to come back, and run off instead to see a big fish or buy a goose."

"That's so," said Jimmy.

"We could sell vegetables and ride around in a high cart," said the Scratch Cat.

"Well that's one way," said the Funny Man, "if you have plenty of vegetables and the high cart."

"I know," said Jimmy, "we can run a lemonade stand. Five cents a glass like the circus."

"And we'd drink all that was left over," said the Scratch Cat.

"That's a first rate plan," said the Funny Man. "And now when you go into business you need capital, so here are two quarters to start on. Take this one and buy some lemons and this one for sugar. But first you go and ask your mothers about it." So off they went. Jimmie's mother was busy fitting a dress on a lady, had her mouth full of pins, but she shook her head yes. And the lady said she'd stop and buy a glass on her way home. So there was a nickel to start with.

The Scratch Cat's mother and Ellen said they would make the lemonade, so the children went running off to the store with the two quarters.

When it was finished it was fine lemonade. The Scratch Cat's mother said they both better drink a glass, so that they could tell customers how good it was. And she said folks who sold lemonade must have very clean hands and not get their thumb in the glass when they poured.

There was a big bucket full with ice floating around. Ellen found a box, which she tipped up sideways, then put a tablecloth on it, then set the glasses in a row in front of the lemonade bucket. The two little stools behind the box were to sit on when you sold to customers. So there they were with their lemonade stand, as fine as could be, out in the grass under the big trees by the road.

"Now I'll yell, just like at a circus," said Jimmy. "Get your ice-cold lemonade, only five cents a glass, whenever I see anybody coming."

"And what will I do?" asked the Scratch Cat.

"You yell too," said Jimmy. So they waited, but nobody came for a long time, then they saw a wagon away down the road. When it got nearer they saw that it was their friend, the Grocery Boy.

"Get your ice-cold lemonade," they yelled together. "Costs you nothing 'cause you are a friend," added the Scratch Cat.

"That's so," said Jimmy. "You couldn't sell to friends." So the Grocery Boy drank a big glass full and said it was fine. But he put a nickel in the money box anyway.

And everyone did that, even the Funny Man, who walked past three times that morning and bought a glass each time. Said he didn't know when he'd been so thirsty.

Then the Scratch Cat's mother, the Politest Child and the baby came walking past and bought a glass for everybody but the baby—it would have curdled him.

More people came along and bought now, and there were lots of nickels—but some boys who sat in the grass threw stones at the lemonade stand because they had only a penny apiece.

So the Scratch Cat felt sorry for them and gave them each a half a glassful and they stopped throwing stones and finally went away.

Then all of a sudden there was an awful noise and barking and running and a pack of dogs came chasing around the corner.

Over went the lemonade and glasses and stools and all the nickels. When the Scratch Cat and Jimmy picked themselves up they knew that the lemonade stand was through with, so they began to hunt the nickels which had rolled every which way. They hunted and hunted and finally found seventeen nickels and three four-leafed clovers, which they divided in two parts, each taking half.

One day the children were playing a pretend game in the Scratch Cat's back yard. But the game was not going very well for the reason that they were not all pretending the same thing. And then the Politest Child didn't like it very well because Jimmy was supposed to kidnap her. You see it was this way, Jimmy was a Goblin, the Scratch Cat was a Witch, and together they were to kidnap the Politest Child, who was to be either a Princess or a Dutchess. They gave her her choice.

About that time the Funny Man came walking along and looked over the fence.

"We are trying to play kidnap," said Jimmy when he saw him.

"Who is to be kidnapped?" asked the Funny Man, leaning on his elbows.

"She is," said the Scratch Cat, pointing at the Politest Child. "Only she won't let the Goblin catch her."

"Who's the Goblin?" asked the Funny Man.

"I am," said Jimmy.

"I don't like it," wailed the Politest Child, "for he kidnaps me by the hair."

The Scratch Cat, who was supposed to be a Witch, said that she would trade, but the Politest Child looked as if she were about to cry, so the Funny Man said that maybe this wasn't a very good day for games, that perhaps they'd better take a walk or something.

"Let's go down and see what Bill the Goat is doing," he said. So that's what they did, all four of them. And the Funny Man bought four bags of popcorn. Bill, who was always obliging, did his two tricks for them and then they gave him their empty popcorn bags, as goats are said to be fond of popcorn bags. Coming up the street the Funny Man asked Jimmy if he watered the telegraph pole regularly. Now as Jimmy wasn't quite sure what regularly meant, he said he'd do it after supper. This probably meant that the Funny Man was going to try to catch another telegram in his hat. It sounded that way anyhow.

The children were excited and wondered what it would be about. Would it be about a goblin and a witch like their game? The Funny Man said "Maybe" again, so they knew. And the last thing that Jimmy did before he went to bed was to pour two sprinklers of water on the telegraph pole though he couldn't understand what it had to do with telegrams. But the Funny Man had said that he should, for poles used to be trees and probably liked it.

Now, as you might know, the three children were on hand bright and early the next morning, eager to know if the Funny Man had caught a telegram in his hat.

Sure enough there he sat on the porch, waving a yellow paper as they came in sight. He said "Hooray," and so did the children, and stood around very close to listen. This is what he read:

To
Mr. and Mrs. Stayaway
Hotel Loafallday
Anyplaceatall.
Foundling left on doorstep. Your child refuses to give it up.

Sophie Frownandscold.

"Well, what does that mean?" asked all the children at once. The Funny Man took off his spectacles and said that he'd tell them the whole story. So here it is.

Once upon a time, not so very long ago there was a Spoiled Child who had something of everything under the Sun. First she had a milk-white pony with such a long trailing tail and mane that they had to be tied up with ribbons. Then she had all manner of toys. Rooms full. Something like a hundred dresses, with hats, shoes and parasols to match. It was too absurd, for there were enough dresses to clothe fifty little girls.

But Sophie Frownandscold was the child's nurse. And no child could be happy with such a nurse. For she said

"Don't do this," and "Don't do that," from morning till night and watched her continually, except such times when she happened to doze off and nap as she sometimes did.

Then there were teachers for all manner of things. One for music, one for dancing, one for books and so on. And they watched her too. So if Sophie and the teachers were not with her there was a groom to keep behind when she went out on the white pony. You see her father and mother were always away doing something they mistook for pleasure, so the poor Spoiled Child was put in the charge of Sophie, all the teachers, the groom, the gardener, and so on. True her parents sent a telegram every day asking about her health and lessons and someone always sent a reply saying that she was both well and studious. But nobody ever said anything about whether she was happy or not.

It will be hard for you to believe it but the poor child had never played with another child, because someone was always on hand to say *no*. And she was told not to speak to strangers or go near the gate for someone might *kidnap* her. Sophie said so, or the teachers said so. Someone was always saying something. However, this child, who had everything, had one pleasure that was *real*. That was reading fairy stories. But not about Fairy Godmothers who waved wands or the meddlesome kind that bossed Cinderella around. *No indeed*, she didn't want to hear about the kind, good Fairies who turn rags into velvets and huts into palaces. She much preferred the goblins and gnomes and witches who hide in queer places and turn people into toads and beggars and other interesting things.

But she was taught out of so many different books, by so many different teachers, and dressed and undressed so many times, that she had few chances to read the fairy book. She was really tired of everything, but most of being told that she might be *kidnapped* some day. She began to wonder if it wouldn't be very nice and the first thing

she knew she was *really* wishing that someone would kidnap her.

Now, every day Sophie went with her into the garden for an airing. She was told to breathe deeply and hold up her head. But it was such a beautiful garden with winding walks and fountains and statues and urns! Like a palace garden. But the Spoiled Child never noticed. She had been through those winding walks with Sophie a hundred times, but she had never *once* played tag there with another child.

Now on this particular day the sun was warm and Sophie, who was fat, felt drowsy, sat down on a marble bench and was soon dozing. Snoring in fact. The Spoiled Child wandered about, glad that no one would say 'don't' for a moment or two. Suddenly she heard a crackling in the shrubbery.

"Maybe I'm going to be kidnapped," she thought. "I'll stand very still so that they can catch me easily." But nothing happened so she parted the leaves to look.

Thereupon she came face to face with a Witch, and a most peculiar looking one. You never could imagine a creature half so curious, though, of course, all witches are born old and wrinkled and rickety.

"Oh, you're a Witch, aren't you?" said the Child in a hushed voice, being careful not to waken Sophie, who would have been frightfully cross about this.

"Certainly I'm a Witch," replied the strange creature.

"Did you ever see a human who looked like me?"

"Then you can help me," said the Spoiled Child.

"That depends on what you want," said the Witch. "Surely you are not going to ask for ponies and toys and such things."

"No," said the Spoiled Child, "but I'd like to be kidnapped."

"That's different," said the Witch, giving her a sharp look. "I'll talk it over with the Goblin."

The Spoiled Child was delighted and forgot and clapped her hands which, of course, wakened Sophie. She sat up in a hurry, rubbed her eyes and immediately began to scold. The Witch vanished in less than a second, the Spoiled Child was hurried to her lessons and nothing else happened that day.

The next day, when it was time to be aired in the garden, the Spoiled Child sat very quietly on the marble bench beside Sophie until she fell asleep and was safely snoring. Then she tiptoed ever so quietly down the winding walk, lifting up and peeping under all the branches and leaves wherever she thought that the little Witch might hide herself. Then finally she found her and the Goblin too.

But if you think that Witches are queer looking you should see a Goblin. My, my!

Well as soon as the Spoiled Child had looked hard enough, the Goblin bowed and the Witch said, "Sit down."

"Where shall I sit?" asked the Spoiled Child.

"On the ground," said the Witch.

"I'm not allowed," said the Child. "I'll take cold or spoil my dress."

"Not at all," said the Witch.

So when the Spoiled Child sat down she saw that the Goblin had a tear in his eye and that the Witch looked rather sad too. Now as you know neither Witches nor Goblins are supposed to be especially kind or good, but rather wicked and mischievous. So these must have been quite different from the usual run for they were so nice and friendly that they were soon calling the Spoiled Child —Sister.

Now, the Goblin was terribly distressed to know that the Child wanted to be kidnapped and that explains why he had a tear on his cheek. But he was clever too, as you shall see, so not a word was said about kidnapping.

"How would you like a playmate, Sister?" asked the Goblin.

"I never had one," said the Child.

"A playmate is better than toys," said the Goblin. And the Witch agreed.

"What kind of a playmate would it be?" asked the Child.

"Either one who wears trousers or one who wears skirts," answered the Goblin.

The Child thought a while, then chose the one that wears trousers.

"Done—that's settled," said the Goblin. "Now the next thing is to prepare his wardrobe of three garments— a shirt, trousers and a roundabout."

"How about shoes and stockings?" asked the Child.

"Foundlings never wear them," said the Goblin.

And of course, just as it was getting interesting Sophie had to wake up from her nap and scream to come at once. She was cross too, and when the Child asked her what a foundling was, she snapped, "A child that is found, of course." Which wasn't an answer at all.

The next day the Child thought airing time would never come and that her dull lessons would never be over, but finally she sat beside Sophie on the marble bench in the sun. And at last Sophie was safely snoring.

Then like a flash the Child was off hunting through the shrubbery for her friends the Witch and the Goblin. Finally she found them behind a hedge sewing away for dear life.

"Here's a thimble, Sister," said the Goblin. "You are to make his shirt."

"But I never made a shirt," said the Spoiled Child, looking surprised.

So the Witch and the Goblin showed her what to do and she was soon sewing as fast as the others. My! but it was fun, really *making* something.

"But how little it must be," said the Child, "to wear such tiny clothes."

"Very small," agreed the Witch.

"How soon will he come?" asked the Child.

"We will fetch him tomorrow, before sun-up," said the Goblin, "and you must be there to open the great door and take him in."

So that night the Spoiled Child scarcely slept at all feeling as other children do the night before Christmas. But of course, this was much nicer, expecting something live to play with, and for whom you had made a tiny shirt yourself.

And as soon as the last stars had faded out, the Child crept down to the door to see if her playmate had come. And sure enough there he was all rolled up in a little ball against the door. Blue eyes, stubby nose, no teeth, the Witch's jacket, the Goblin's trousers—and her shirt! My, how she squealed and laughed and danced around for it was so much nicer than anything that she ever had before. Then upstairs she flew with her tiny treasure and dropped it in the middle of her soft white bed. And that's where Sophie Frownandscold found them later, the Spoiled Child and the Foundling playing together.

As you might imagine it caused a great stir in the big house for Sophie did a great deal of loud talking and the spectacled teachers were shaking their heads and saying that something must be done about the blue-eyed, stubby-nosed Foundling. So they all decided—Sophie and the teachers that the Foundling must go—*it must go at once.*

And they sent a telegram, the very one that the Funny Man had read—and told the Spoiled Child's parents what a shocking thing had happened. But they little dreamed that it would never reach them but would drop off the wires into an old man's hat.

Neither did they guess that a telegram had *already* gone to those far-away-parents. The clever Goblin had sent one which read like this:

Return at once. Something has happened.

Goblin and Witch Kidnappers.

"Now, that will start them home," he chuckled. And the Witch agreed that it would. And it did. The next day they came home—boxes and trunks, all excited. But when things finally quieted down and Sophie and the spectacled teachers stood waiting to see the Foundling sent away, a strange thing happened.

"I think I'll not be kidnapped," said the Spoiled Child, "for I like it better now that the Goblin and the Witch brought me a playmate. So I think I'll stay."

"Of course you'll stay," said her Father.

"Of course," said her Mother.

"And the Foundling?" asked Sophie.

"He's a *playmate*, not a Foundling," said the Child, "and he belongs to *me* because I made him a shirt. He's *mine*."

"That settles it," said the Father. And the Mother agreed. Very much disgusted Sophie and the spectacled teachers flounced out of the room.

So that's how it happened that the Playmate came to live in the big house with the Child who was not really spoiled—only lonely.

Then one day she told her Father that she wanted something *very* much.

And he said, "What can it be?"

"A pretty little house in the garden where a Witch and a Goblin can live," said the Child. So the Father had the prettiest little house built that anyone ever saw, with windows, a stove and chimney, everything in fact. And over the door was a sign which read, "Goblin and Witch, Kidnappers."

And that was their house whenever they wanted it, and nowadays the Child and her playmate spend most of the time playing together in the beautiful garden.

The next thing to happen was a wedding. Everybody was talking about it but most particularly the Politest Child, because she was in it. The Scratch Cat and Jimmy weren't, though. But Jimmy's mother was making the bride's dresses and one of the Boarding House Ladies was making the bride's cake and everybody was giving her a present, even though it wasn't Christmas.

The bride played the organ in Sunday School and was the Politest Child's music teacher—which was why *she* was in the wedding. So the Scratch Cat said. And it was to be in the church and everyone was to wear his best clothes. But the Funny Man, Jimmy and the Scratch Cat weren't invited. Of course, afterward there would be a party—with a cake like that, and ice cream, too, Jimmy thought.

The Politest Child had new slippers and a new white dress and a sash and talked a great deal about carrying a basket of flowers. In fact, everybody was talking about it except Jimmy and the Scratch Cat.

The bride came every day to Jimmy's house and tried on dresses and dresses, and Jimmy thought that she looked like an angel in a white one with flying things like wings, and flowers in her hair. My! Jimmy wished he were going to the wedding. And the Scratch Cat wished so, too.

Then the day came and the cake was ready to send and the Boarding House Ladies let Jimmy and the Scratch Cat and the Funny Man see it. If you'll believe it, there was a little doll on top dressed like a bride and there were doves and flowers made of frosting, and it was *huge* and as white as snow. Of course it made them wish more than ever that they were going.

As everyone was busier than usual that day Jimmy and the Scratch Cat thought that they would go back in the alley and see Jeff.

"Maybe he's going, too," said Jimmy.

"We'll ask him," said the Scratch Cat.

But Jeff said "No, indeed!" He wasn't going to any wedding, not when there was a county fair the same day.

"Is a county fair like a circus?" asked Jimmy.

"Well sort of," said Jeff.

"I never went to one," said the Scratch Cat.

"Neither did I," said Jimmy, "but I'd like to."

Then what do you suppose Jeff said? Why, he said, "All right, come on, it's not very far."

Now you know that Jimmy wasn't allowed to run off like that, and of course the Scratch Cat wasn't, either. But it didn't take a minute for them to climb up into the buggy when Jeff said, "Get in."

Off through the alley they went, pell mell, and around corners till the first thing they knew they were away out in the country.

"Want to drive?" asked Jeff.

"Yes, yes," said Jimmy and the Scratch Cat, wriggling with delight.

So they took turns holding the lines and slapping them up and down on the horse's broad back to make him go faster. They were sure that they had *never* had such a good time.

"There's the fair grounds," said Jeff, pointing with the whip. People were standing around everywhere looking at horses and cows and pigs and chickens that were behind a fence. Then there were the biggest pumpkins that ever grew, and fancy bed quilts hung up—and oh, everything!

"I can't see anything," said the Scratch Cat finally, for you see she was being squeezed and pushed away down in the crowd.

"Here you go," said Jeff, and he swung her up on his shoulder so she could look over all the heads.

"There's the Balloon Man," she squealed.

"Where?" said poor Jimmy, who couldn't see at all, though he could hear the squawking. So Jeff pushed and pushed till they finally stood beside the frowsy fellow who held a big bunch of red and blue and green balloons and the noisy kind, too, which grown-ups do not like.

Then Jeff bought one for each of them—a red one for the Scratch Cat and Jimmy's was blue. Then he counted the money that was left and bought peanuts and lemonade for all of them.

"Haven't any more money now," said Jeff, "so I guess we'd better be going home."

"I don't want to go home," said the Scratch Cat.

"Neither do I," said Jimmy.

"Your folks will think you are lost," said Jeff.

"No, they won't," said the Scratch Cat. "They are at the wedding."

But Jeff was worried, anyway, so they got back into the buggy and started home. When they turned into the alley and stopped in front of the livery stable, there stood the Funny Man.

"I know where you've been," he said, looking at the

balloons. Jeff said something about being sorry, but the children weren't sorry, for they had had a very good time.

"Everybody is at the wedding," said the Funny Man, "and I won't tell on you this time." So they said good-bye to Jeff and thanked him for the balloons and peanuts and everything.

Jimmy and the Scratch Cat were counting their lemon-ade-stand nickels. The Scratch Cat had spent the most and had only three left while Jimmy had five. She had bought candy and popcorn and had given several at Sunday School, while Jimmy had bought colored pencils and a drawing book.

"Well, let's earn some more money," said Jimmy.

"How?" asked the Scratch Cat.

Jimmy rolled his eyes. "A vegetable garden," he said finally because he couldn't think of anything else.

"All right," said the Scratch Cat. "Let's."

Of course they went down to talk it over with the Funny Man, and he said that it wouldn't hurt to try, so they went to the store and bought seeds with some of their nickels.

The Scratch Cat's mother helped them to plant the seeds in neat rows, then they watered them with Jimmy's green sprinkling can, but there was nothing to do but wait for the vegetables slow as they were.

So they decided to earn some more nickels picking blackberries that grew along the side of the road. The Scratch Cat's mother bought as many as they could pick and made pies of them. Pretty soon though they had picked all that grew anywhere about. So one day the Grocery Boy said that they could ride along with him to the country where he was taking a basket. But first they asked their mothers as the Funny Man had said they must.

The Grocery Boy was very nice indeed. He could whistle louder than anyone in town. He said so himself. He ran in with baskets of groceries to different houses and out again so fast that big gray Mike hardly stopped at all.

They went that way every day and the Grocery Boy said that Mike knew the places to leave baskets as well as he did himself. When all the baskets were left, they turned into a little road where the blackberries were *thick*, and they all picked and ate as fast as they could. And if you'll believe it they got a big grocery basket full. The Boarding

House Ladies bought these blackberries and gave them each a quarter.

Then one morning, when they were looking around the garden where the seeds were, they saw a tiny green leaf, then another and another.

"Radishes," said Jimmy.

That's what they were, so they ran down to see the Funny Man and tell him that the vegetable garden had started. And he said that he'd buy all of the radishes that they had because they were his favorite vegetables.

As the radishes were still very small and would have to stay in the ground for several weeks they decided to make some money by having a circus.

"We'll sell tickets to people," said the Scratch Cat.

"Who will be in the circus?" asked Jimmy.

"Dandelion can do tricks," said the Scratch Cat. "And the Popcorn Man's goat and the parrot can be in it too." So off they went down the street to see about it.

"Please will you let your goat be in a circus?" said Jimmy. The Pop-corn Man looked surprised.

"Whose circus?" he asked.

"Ours," said the Scratch Cat.

That made a big difference and he said, "Yes," because they were such good customers.

"All right then! Come on, Bill," said Jimmy, taking hold of the goat's collar. But what do you suppose that goat did? He lay *down* and wouldn't move an inch. Not an inch.

"I guess he isn't a circus goat," said Jimmy. And the Pop-corn Man said he guessed he wasn't. So that settled that.

"Let's find out about the parrot then," said the Scratch Cat. So they crossed the street to the fruit stand.

"Please can your parrot be in our circus?" asked Jimmy very politely.

The fruit stand man laughed and gave them each a big plum. Then he whistled for the parrot and told him to come out from under the counter where he was hiding. But the parrot was cross and snapped at their fingers and wouldn't talk.

So they decided not to have the circus at all. When they told the Funny Man about it he said the best way to have a circus is to do all the tricks yourself then you'll know that they are well done.

"How would you like to have a sea-saw?" he asked.

"We'd *like* it," said both children at once.

"All right," said the Funny Man. "Come along." They went into the garden behind the boarding house and the Funny Man got things out of the woodshed and almost before they knew it he had the sea-saw all fixed and they were riding up and down on it.

They decided that as soon as they could sea-saw like real circus people they'd begin to sell tickets. But the Funny Man said he thought that they'd better stick to garden truck and he gave them all the nickels he had in his pockets and told them to deliver *his* radishes as soon as they were ripe.

One day the children found Ellen sitting out in the grass drying her long hair in the sun while the baby took his nap.

"Ellen looks like a fairy," said Jimmy, "because her hair ripples in the sunshine."

"Good fairy, or bad fairy?" asked the Scratch Cat.

"Good, of course," said Jimmy.

"Let's get her to tell us a fairy story, then," said the Politest Child. So they asked her, but like all grown-ups, except the Funny Man, she said that she didn't know any.

But they kept right on teasing, so Ellen, who was kind, finally said she'd try, if they would tell her what they wanted the story to be about.

"About a fat queen," said the Scratch Cat who liked funny stories.

"Oh, no," said the Politest Child. "Tell one about a fairy who lived in a castle."

Ellen thought that that sounded interesting and so did the children, so everybody sat down close together.

"Well, once upon a time there was a lovely fairy who lived with her step-father in a lonely castle far up in the mountains. The step-father wasn't a fairy himself, but a Highwayman and no better than he should be. But he never guessed that she was a fairy and he made her work from morning till night. You see, her mother, who was also a fairy, had long since floated away like a bit of thistle-down, leaving the poor child behind to get along as best she might.

"Now, it was clear to the fairy that her wicked step-father was robbing everybody who came that way. For the dungeon was well filled with wretched prisoners and the tower was fairly bristling with sacks of gold. But the big doors leading into these places were always kept locked and the keys dangling from the wicked Highwayman's girdle, so what was one small fairy to do?

"As you will guess, this was a most dreadful place to live, for the unfortunate prisoners in the dungeon continually pounded on the big door and that made the fairy shudder and shake. But every day the rogue would set out

to rob someone, coming back at night with all manner of things. If his luck was good he would feed the prisoners generously, but if not, so much the worse for them.

"Now, perhaps you never knew it, but tea-kettles talk, and if you are wise you will soon discover that they can tell you a great deal. Indeed, the fairy's tea-kettle was the only cheerful thing in the big gloomy castle for it chuckled and sang all day long. And they talked together as a brother and sister would talk and so passed many a lonely hour.

"Well, one stormy night the Highwayman came home in a black mood, for he had prowled the forest all day and found no one to rob.

"'Food, and be quick about it!' he bellowed at the fairy as he entered the castle. So she flew here and there in great haste to serve him, but nothing suited and his manners and temper grew steadily worse. Then to make matters really bad, he reached for the great keys to the dungeon and the tower and discovered that they were *gone*. Then, as you might know, he raged furiously up and down as only a Highwayman can.

"Of course the poor fairy hadn't an idea what to do— *goodness knows* she had had nothing to do with the keys! So she hid herself in the cupboard among the pots and pans, but she trembled so that they soon began to rattle and jingle most alarmingly. Finally the Highwayman heard the commotion and stopped to listen.

"'What can it be?' he said to himself. 'Surely not the prisoners banging on the dungeon door!' Now you may not know it, but such rogues as this Highwayman are cowards as well, and the sound of the pots and pans jingling in the cupboard soon set him to trembling. He fancied that it was an evil spirit come to punish him, so he crept stealthily off to bed and covered up his head to shut out the sound.

"And if you'll believe it the little tea-kettle on the

hearth laughed until it almost boiled over. Of course, this reached the ears of the scared little fairy hiding in the cupboard, and she poked her head out, very carefully.

" 'What *can* you find to laugh about?' she asked.

" 'Everything is *so* funny,' chuckled the tea-kettle.

" 'I wish that I thought so, too,' said the poor fairy.

" 'You see, I know where the Highwayman's keys are,' sputtered the tea-kettle.

" 'No!' said the Fairy.

" 'Yes!' said the tea-kettle.

" 'Tell me where!' said the Fairy.

" 'Rolled up in the rug where he dropped them,' said the tea-kettle. 'I'll puff some steam right at the very spot.'

"But just then the Highwayman uncovered his head and sat up.

" 'Begin to tremble,' hissed the tea-kettle. So the Fairy trembled with all her might and very soon the pots and pans started to rattle and jingle.

" 'Save me!' cried the cowardly Highwayman, and buried his face again in the pillow.

" 'Now,' bubbled the tea-kettle. 'While I fill the room with steam you run for the keys, unlock the dungeon and free all the prisoners.'

"So, quick as a flash the Fairy flew toward the big keys where they had dropped on the rug, then down to the dungeon door. It was all she could do to lift the great key and turn it, but finally it was done and the door swung open.

"My what a sight! Prisoners and prisoners! First came a fat Queen saying, 'I told you so,' to the King.

" 'Told me what?' snapped the King, who was hungry.

" 'I told you that a good fairy would come to help us out. And here she is,' said the Queen.

" 'Introduce her to the Prince,' said the King. 'She deserves it.'

"So then and there the lovely fairy met the fair young Prince. And you could guess the rest of the story for yourselves, probably, if the tea-kettle hadn't boiled over just then.'

"'Oh, Oh!' said the Fairy.

"'What's the matter?' asked the Prince.

"'Too late, too late,' whistled the tea-kettle. 'While you were getting introduced the Highwayman escaped.'

"'Well who cares?' said the King. 'Let's have some supper.' So the Queen and the Fairy rolled up their sleeves and prepared a great feast for all the prisoners. My, what a merry party it was! But you can't guess who laughed the most. The tea-kettle of course! Well, as you might know the lovely Fairy and the young Prince were married and on their wedding day they took the great key and unlocked the tower room where all the sacks of gold were stored. Each prisoner was given as much as he could carry away, so not only the bride and groom but everyone else lived happily ever after."

*   *   *   *   *

"And what became of the tea-kettle?" asked the Scratch Cat.

"Oh," said Ellen, "the fairy took it with her wherever she went because it was such a clever kettle and always saw the funny side of things."

Now one day Jimmy was in the sewing room with his mother drawing colored pictures. "Now what color shall I make the horse and what color shall I make the cart?" Then she'd tell him. But after a while, because she was cutting out, she told him to look out of the window and see something, then make a picture like it.

"Well, I see a horse and a man and a tree," said Jimmy.

"How about a leaf?" asked his mother.

"There goes one now," said Jimmy. "Just dropped off the tree." So he hurried downstairs and caught it before it could blow away. It was all yellow and red and had a jiggley pointed edge all around.

His mother thought it was lovely so he decided to make the picture for her and give it to her to hang up over the work table. And so he was *very* particular and it got prettier and prettier and she thought that it was beautiful too. And sure enough she pinned it up where she could see it all day.

He decided to draw another leaf, even better, but just then the door bell rang, and Jimmy went flying down to see who was there. Of course, he loved to open the door and say, "How-do-you-do!" And there stood such a very pretty lady that Jimmy said, "Come in" right away without saying "How-do-you-do" first. So she went up the steps and Jimmy thought that she wore very pretty slippers.

Then she sat down and talked to his mother about a new dress. She was a school teacher. She said so. She didn't look as if she would ever be cross and scold either.

Then she looked at Jimmie's leaf picture and said that it was *very good* and that after a while when he went to school maybe he could draw on the blackboard with colored chalk. Think of that.

Well, after the pretty school teacher got through talking about her new dress and went out the door, Jimmy said, "I know Mother what I want to do."

Mother said, "What?"

"I want to go to school!"

She said she'd see about it, and that maybe he could before long. So Jimmy went over to ask the Funny Man what he thought about it. He found him on the porch, so Jimmy sat down on the top step, just as he always did when there was something to be talked over.

"I want to go to school," he said.

"Well you *are* getting to be a big boy," answered the Funny Man.

"What is school like?" asked Jimmy after a while.

"I almost forget," answered the Funny Man. "But you'll have to learn to spell and add and read out of your primer. And you must not whisper, or be tardy!"

"Please tell me a story about a boy that went to school," said Jimmy.

"Well—let—me—see," said the Funny Man thinking. "All right," he said finally, "here's one about Tardy Peter."

"Once upon a time there was a little boy who was always late. He was the last one going to bed at night and the last one getting up in the morning. He was tardy at school every day, late to his meals and behind in his lessons.

"His name was Peter but everyone who knew him called him Tardy Peter. But beside being always late, he was what the neighbors called—*queer*.

"And you'll think so too when I tell you that Tardy Peter had a pet cricket that lived—where? You'll *never* guess. In his pocket. Yes, sir. It was only a little cricket and quite handsome as crickets go. And not common at all like vegetable garden crickets. No, indeed. This one called itself a 'pocket-cricket' and looked down on all other crickets. But aside from being something of a snob he had few faults and many virtues.

"Now, Tardy Peter went to school, that is, he started every morning, but something always happened along the way to make him late. The Teacher kept the names of all the girls and boys on the black-board, but after poor Peter's name was a long row of red marks which meant that he had been tardy that many times. And of course this worried the Teacher, his Mother, and Peter, as well.

"The Teacher was almost cross because there were so many red marks. And Peter's mother was getting very sad and wondered *what* was to be done about it.

"And all Peter could say was that he didn't know, for he guessed he couldn't help being late. You see, he'd forget all about school and go chasing rabbits and butterflies and hunting birds' nests and things like that.

"But the worst of it was he didn't know what the lessons were about, couldn't find the place and was always at the foot of his class. So you see, something had to be done with Tardy Peter.

"Then someone said that it must be the fault of the pet cricket, for other children without pet crickets were never tardy. That surely was the explanation. His mother thought so, the Teacher thought so, everyone thought so. And they talked it over and decided that he would have to give the cricket away if he were late again.

"Now, of course, the cricket heard all this and it made him very nervous, indeed, for he couldn't think of living in anyone's else pocket but Tardy Peter's. As for getting along without his pet, Peter would rather have had all of the red tardy marks in the world.

" 'Something must be done,' said the cricket.

" 'That's what they all say,' answered Peter.

" 'What shall we do, anyway?' asked the cricket, looking sad.

" 'I'm sure I don't know,' said Peter.

" 'I have an idea,' said the cricket after a while.

" 'What is it?' asked Peter.

" 'I'll be an alarm-cricket.'

" 'A what?'

" 'Let me explain,' said the cricket. 'Whenever you are going to be late, and forget what you ought to do, I'll go off just like an alarm clock and scare you back again.'

" 'All right,' said Peter. 'When do we begin?'

" 'The next time you are late,' said the cricket.

" 'All right,' said Peter and began to read in his big animal book.

" 'Bed time, Peter,' said his Mother, opening the door.

" 'Just a minute more,' said Peter, going on with the bear story.

" 'Past bed time,' said his Mother a half an hour later.

" 'Just let me finish this story, please.' But just then

there was a noise like a crow and a squeak and a whistle all together. The book fell on the floor and Peter jumped up, said goodnight and went running off to bed.

" 'Well, well,' said his Mother. 'What happened to Peter?'

"But the next morning when Peter's mother called him and he turned over and covered up his head, he heard that queer noise again.

" 'Hello,' he said. 'There's my Alarm Cricket.' So he jumped out of bed and hopped into his clothes in a hurry.

" 'Hooray!' said the cricket. And Peter said 'Hooray!' too.

" 'Well, well, what has happened to Peter?' said all the family when he came down to breakfast on time. And be fore the day was over everybody was saying 'What *has* happened to Peter?' For, you see, he got to school on time, had all his lessons like the other boys and girls and everything worked like a charm.

"Now the next day something did happen that very nearly—but wait and hear about it.

"Peter started off to school just when the clock said that he should, but on the way he met a loose horse coming down the road.

"The Horse stopped, looked down his long nose and said, 'Good morning, Peter.'

" 'Good morning,' answered Peter.

" 'Nice day,' said the Horse.

"Peter said, 'Yes, it is.'

" 'Let's go for a ride, over the hills and far away,' said the Horse.

" 'I have to go to school,' said Peter.

" 'Climb up on my back, I'll take you to school,' said the Horse. So Peter gave a big jump, landed on the Horse's back and off they went.

"But when they drew near the school house Peter was having such a fine time that he never noticed where they were. And the Horse was telling his life story and didn't notice, either. It seems that when he was young he was a fire department horse and helped pull the hose-cart. He was very proud of that and seemed to enjoy telling about it, and how quick he was when he heard the fire alarm. So they went galloping on far down the road at a great pace.

"Then all of a sudden there was that queer noise—a crow and a squeak and a whistle, all together.

" 'Gracious!' said the Horse, stopping suddenly. 'What *was* that? It sounded like the fire alarm.'

" 'It's for me,' said Peter. 'I'm going to be late to school. Please take me back.'

" 'Of course,' said the Horse. 'That would never do.' So he turned around and rushed back at a terrible speed and just as the tardy bell sounded Peter slid down and ran into the school house.

"So the days passed and the faithful cricket continued to sound the alarm so that Peter was never, *never* late to bed, or to breakfast and had no more red tardy marks after his name. And best of all he was at the head of the class.

"Now, of course, everybody was pleased and wondered how it had all happened. So Peter told them about his alarm-cricket and how he had taught him to be on time. And to reward the cricket suitably all of Peter's friends fed him so many good things that very soon he was too fat to ride around in Peter's pocket. So they made him a nice little home in the clock which thereafter was never known to be even *one* minute late."

*　*　*　*　*

"So there you are, Jimmy," said the Funny Man, "and don't forget about the tardy marks.

"I won't," said Jimmy. Then the Funny Man asked if the Scratch Cat was going to school too. But as Jimmy didn't know he said he'd go and see, so he started up the street toward her house.

As the Scratch Cat kept right on having measles, Jimmy had no one to play with except the Funny Man. Well, one day they started off to do something. Anything at all.

"Let's go back through the alley and see Jeff," said Jimmy. "I'll tell him that I'm going to school." They found Jeff sitting in a comfortable chair tipped back against the livery stable.

"Hello," they said.

And Jeff said, "Take a chair."

As there were two more chairs they sat down and Jimmy thought that he would tip too, when suddenly his chair slipped out from under him and his head hit the ground *hard*.

"Now I guess I'm going to cry," he said to himself. But just then he heard the Funny Man say, "Fellows don't cry."

So he didn't. But it hurt.

Then to make him stop thinking about his head the Funny Man said, "Let's go down and look at the ships." Of course he *knew* that Jimmy would rather do that than anything else.

Jeff had to watch the livery stable so he couldn't go along. But he said to "Come back again," and they said they would.

Now it's queer the way ships make you feel, isn't it? As if you had been away off somewhere yourself. Jimmy liked the way they smelled, too—of tar. The Funny Man knew just where to go and he called everyone they met "Captain." And as they were all friendly Jimmy and the Funny Man sat down on a bench with some of the Captains.

"Come here, young fellow," said the big Captain, with the red face. So Jimmy sat on his knee and he asked him how he'd like to go aboard.

"I'd like it," said Jimmy. So they climbed down a ladder and got on a boat that was tied to the dock. Jimmy thought that it looked like the picture of Noah's Ark in Sunday School.

Then the big Captain took him into his cabin and showed him lots of things and he gave him a shell that roared when he held it up to his ear.

"What's that?" said Jimmy, pointing up at a shelf.

And the big Captain took it down and told Jimmy that he could have that too. It was a little wooden elephant with a tail and a trunk and everything that real elephants have. He said that it had come from away off where elephants live in the woods. Monkeys, too. Think of that.

Then they climbed back up the ladder and another Captain gave Jimmy a turtle, a little one, that could pull himself all inside his shell, so it looked as if he wasn't there at all.

Jimmy was pleased and he thanked all the kind Captains over and over. The Funny Man carried the turtle for him, but Jimmy carried the roaring shell in one hand and the little wooden elephant in the other. It was almost like Christmas, and he hopped most of the way home on one foot, just because he was so happy.

"Do you know any stories about little elephants?" asked Jimmy.

"Yes, I think I do know one about a little boy elephant," said the Funny Man.

So here it is just as Jimmy heard it.

"Once upon a time there was a little boy elephant who lived in a big dark woods, where the trees were so tall that you couldn't see the tops of them, and where the leaves were so thick that even the monkeys had never counted them. But it was a very nice place for little animals to live, and they all liked it very much. There were little lions and tigers and elephants and leopards that could climb just any place *at all*, and there was a young giraffe who could look over all the heads of the other animals. But the monkeys were far the smartest of course, for they could talk and do tricks.

"Now this little boy elephant admired all the other animals very much indeed and felt awfully ashamed when he thought about himself for there wasn't anything he could do but make big round footprints in the mud—not another thing.

"He used to say to himself, 'Here I am with this crazy long nose that only gets in my way when I try to run and is really no good *at all*. None of the other animals have anything of the sort.' And his big fan shaped ears worried him and his clubby feet and his muddy skin. He was very blue about himself—that little boy elephant.

"Now there was a very nice Lady Monkey who lived in the woods and she knew more about everything than all the other animals put together. And beside knowing so much, she had the prettiest monkey baby that ever was. It was everybody's pet. Even the stuck-up lions liked it.

"The little boy elephant used to take care of the Lady Monkey's baby sometimes when she was busy reading or something. So occasionally he'd tell her how blue he was and cry a little about his crazy long nose and fan shaped ears and all the rest that worried him so much.

"But sensible woman that she was, she would tell him to cheer up, that very likely there was some good reason why he had a nose like that and such ears and feet and complexion. *Wait and see!*

"As you know that was good advice for usually there

is some good reason for things that cannot be helped. So the little boy elephant decided that he *would* wait and see and maybe sometime he'd understand.

"Well one day the little boy elephant was rocking the Lady Monkey's baby in its hammock of grape vines and singing 'rock-a-bye baby on the tree top' when suddenly he heard something.

" 'Hark,' he said, twisting one big fan shaped ear into place. Then the other one.

"Now that little boy elephant was much smarter than anyone knew, even himself!

"So he squatted down to wait and see, and he made himself look exactly like a big brown stone. No one would ever have guessed that it was an elephant. Then he spread his long nose out on the ground and made it look exactly like the root of a tree. You never would have known that it was an elephant's trunk. 'Now then,' he said to himself.

"And the next thing that happened along came a wicked old organ grinder creeping through the trees. Enough to scare anybody. The little boy elephant watched him out of the corner of one eye. Nearer and nearer he came. He meant of course to steal the pretty monkey baby. Organ grinders always have them, you know, to pass the penny cup.

"But the first thing that that wicked organ grinder knew he stumbled over a root that suddenly straightened out and wrapped itself around him, *tight*. Then a big brown stone stood up and a big round foot cuffed him first on one ear, then on the other.

"My, but that organ grinder did yell! Then all the other animals hearing the racket came running to see what on earth was happening. But the little boy elephant kept right on cuffing away with his big round foot.

" 'That's almost enough',' said the Lady Monkey, who had come rushing home when she heard the noise.

" 'Will you promise never to steal another baby?' demanded the little boy elephant.

" 'Cross my heart,' bawled the organ grinder, 'Never! Never! Never!'

"So they told him to begone and never come back even to play a tune on his grind organ.

" 'Now,' said the Lady Monkey. 'Didn't I tell you that there was some good reason why you have a long nose and big ears and round feet and a muddy complexion?'

" 'I see now,' said the little boy elephant. So he never complained about anything anymore."

"What became of him when he grew up into a big elephant?" asked Jimmy.

"He probably joined a circus," said the Funny Man.

*   *   *   *   *

"Now let's talk about the turtle," said Jimmy.

"All right," said the Funny Man. "But what that little turtle needs is a box of sand and a puddle to swim in."

"Maybe he could live in the Scratch Cat's sand pile. Let's go and see," said Jimmy.

So they went up the street to her house and there she was sitting by the window, wrapped up in a quilt and looking out.

"I'm well again," she called as soon as she saw them.

Jimmy and the Funny Man said, "That's fine."

Then she leaned out and asked what they had. So they showed her the turtle which was just a little thing, but it could pull itself all inside so that you'd never guess that a turtle was there at all.

"Can it live in your sand pile?" asked Jimmy. And the Scratch Cat's mother said, "Of course it can." So the Funny Man made a little place in the sand and fixed a pan of water in the middle, then he built a fence of stone all around so that the turtle couldn't run away, and that's where it was to live.

The Scratch Cat sat by the window to watch and her mother said that tomorrow she could go outside. Then the next day after that she and Jimmy would start to school.

The next morning early, Jimmy went up to see how the turtle was. He found the Scratch Cat, Dandelion and the Politest Child all watching it swimming round and round the pan. Dandelion didn't know what to make of it at all, and would start to put a foot in, then pull it back in a hurry.

"Let's take the turtle to school with us tomorrow," said Jimmy.

"And Dandelion too," said the Scratch Cat.

"Only *babies* do that," said the Politest Child. "And you'll get sent home—but you have to come home at recess anyway because you're only beginners."

"Who cares?" said the Scratch Cat proudly. "We're going to start anyway if we are beginners." It was so exciting just thinking about it that they could hardly get their dinners. Even the Funny Man was excited and said like as not he'd go himself.

Finally it was the next morning and Scratch Cat and Jimmy were ready in their new school clothes. And what do you suppose? The Funny Man came bringing a fine school bag to Jimmy. It was just like the one that they had given the Scratch Cat when she had the measles only it was blue. And it said on it, "For a good boy."

Then the school bell rang.

"Come on, come on," said both the children, "Or we'll be late." You see they hadn't forgotten about "Tardy Peter."

So they started. The Scratch Cat's mother went along to show them the way and tell the teacher all about them.

In through the big doors they marched with all the other children. And there were rooms on both sides as you walked along, and you could see children sitting in rows or marching, and in some of the rooms they were singing.

Finally they stopped at the last room of all, and the teacher said "Come in." What do you suppose? Why it was the same pretty teacher that had come to Jimmie's house to get a dress. Yes, sir, the *very one*.

"How do you do, Jimmy," said the Teacher. Then she said, "And how do you do, Mary," because that was the Scratch Cat's real name.

So they sat down with the other children, and each one had a little seat and a desk. And there were blackboards all around the room with beautiful colored chalk pictures. The Teacher told them lots of things *not to do*, like wiggling and whispering and looking around. She gave them each a primer to keep and it had pictures and big printed words in it.

Then after a while it was time for the beginners to go home, so they stood up and marched when the Teacher told them, and put on their hats and went out with all the other children. But they didn't want to go home *at all*. But when they turned the last corner they saw some one waiting. You can guess who it was of course. The Funny Man had come to meet them and he called them by their school names—James and Mary—just for fun.

"Let's get some ice cream," he said. "Because it's the first day of school."

"Let's," said the children.

So they did—ten cent dishes of vanilla all around.

The children felt as if they had been away from home for a long time.

"How's Dandelion?" asked Jimmy.

"And how's the Turtle?" asked the Scratch Cat.

The Funny Man said they were about the same. Then they told him about their side by side seats, the blackboard pictures and how pretty the teacher was.

But there were lots and lots more days, just like the first one, and if you'll believe it the time came when the children could write their own names and read out of their primers.

One day Scratch Cat and Jimmy came from school all excited. "We must have false faces and Jack-o-lanterns to scare folks with Hallowe'en," they told Jimmy's mother. "Whom are you going to scare?" she wanted to know. "Everybody but you," they told her.

She told them to keep it a secret, so all the folks would be *surprised*, and that's why they didn't tell the Funny Man or the Boarding House Ladies or anybody. But they *did* tell Jeff, of course, because they wanted him to help them make Jack-o-lanterns. And as you might know Jeff thought that it was a fine idea and said, "Yes, I can make tick-tacks too!"

But how to get pumpkins, because there weren't any in the Scratch Cat's vegetable garden! Finally Jeff said, "I know where!" And he hitched up a livery stable horse to one of the buggies and off they went in a hurry over the country roads. In the fields along the way the corn stalks were stacked up like Indian wigwams and in between the rows there were pumpkins and *pumpkins*. But they were all on the other side of the fence and Jeff said that *that* would be stealing to take one. Then what do you think. As they were driving along they saw a little pumpkin that had crowded through the fence and was out in the road. Just as much as to say, "Here I am, make a Jack-o-lantern out of me."

"Whoa," said Jeff, and Jimmy was out in a minute after that pumpkin which was round and smooth and all that a pumpkin should be. Now the next thing was to get another one just as nice and growing, of course, outside the fence. So they drove and *drove* watching both sides of the fence at once. It certainly didn't look as if any other little pumpkins had crawled out into the road hoping to be somebody's Jack-o-lantern. Jeff looked worried and said that he didn't have any money along to buy one, and the children had just enough in their banks at home to buy false faces. There were any number of pumpkins that looked as if just a tiny little shove would push them *under* the fence. But shoving would be stealing, so they drove on.

"There it is," said the Scratch Cat. And before the others even saw it, she jumped out of the buggy and was across the road.

It took a big push to get it into the buggy beside the other one. Then they hurried home and Jeff began to cut pumpkin faces, right there in the alley. All the folks passing by stopped and watched. It made you laugh to look at them, but after dark when they were lit up they looked *very* fierce.

The next thing was to get false faces. So the Scratch Cat and Jimmy shook the nickels out of their banks and went running to the store to pick out the three funniest ones that there were.

On the way home they met the Funny Man.

"What are you children up to?" he asked.

"It's to be a secret," said Jimmy.

"No it isn't," said the Scratch Cat. "It's a surprise."

"Is that *so?*" said the Funny Man.

Then finally it was dark and everything was ready. As

Jimmie's mother was in the secret, she helped them get fixed up in their false faces, with sunbonnets on their heads, and old shawls and things wrapped around them.

"Now let's scare the Funny Man and the Boarding House Ladies first," said Jimmy. So they ran across the street and tiptoed up on the front porch which was all dark. And right then something happened. A big ghost with a plug hat and a false face jumped out of a corner and flapped its long white arms and made awful noises. How they ran! Scratch Cat and Jimmy almost dropped their Jack-o-lanterns and their sunbonnets flew off and they never stopped till they heard Jeff laugh.

Then they laughed too when they saw that it was the Funny Man all fixed up to scare *them*. But you *never* would have known him. But that's the way it always is on Hallowe'en. The wrong people always get scared.

Then the Funny Man said that maybe they'd better surprise the Boarding House Ladies as long as they were

all fixed up to scare somebody. So the four of them went creeping around the house to the back door throwing corn at all the windows. My, but those ladies were surprised when they opened the door and saw those four false faces and Jack-o-lanterns looking at them. But as soon as they got over it they passed doughnuts and apples which people are *supposed* to eat at Hallowe'en.

So the next thing was to go up and surprise all the folks at the Scratch Cat's house. It *was* fine there because they squealed and pulled down the blinds and made a great fuss. After a while the Scratch Cat's mother opened the door and asked them to come in. And she let on, and all the others did, too, that they didn't know who they were and said funny things about how they looked. Then more apples and doughnuts were passed, and since you cannot eat when you have a false face on they had to take them off. So then all the surprises were over.

Jimmy and the Scratch Cat now stayed at school all day and came home when the big boys and girls did, so nobody called them "beginners" any more. Of course they had recess now, which is one of the nicest things about school. But the Scratch Cat and Jimmy couldn't play together—for he had to play over in the boys' yard, and you know they had the *most* fun over there—because girls whisper so much about their dresses and their dolls and things like that. So the Scratch Cat would rather have played with the boys. Even the little boys played football too, just like the big ones, and wore rough sweaters.

But one day a new girl came to school and she was different from all the other ones, for she could cut pictures with scissors—birds and horses, and she could jump higher than any of the boys. Her name was Hilda, and the Scratch Cat liked her right away. Hilda had round blue eyes, a stubby nose and yellow hair, and if the boys teased her she'd chase them and grab their hats.

At home the Scratch Cat talked a great deal about Hilda and the wonderful things that she could do, and what good little cakes she brought to school at recess. Then one day she told her Mother that Hilda wanted them—Jimmy too, to come to her house after school. But nobody seemed to know anything about Hilda, or where she lived or where she came from. Nobody but the Scratch Cat who kept saying how nice and different Hilda was, how high she could jump, and so on. Then one day they came home together and the Scratch Cat's mother liked Hilda too, and said that she might go. And Jimmy was allowed too, so off the three children started. But it was a long way, nearly down to the ships. You see Hilda's father was a sailor and she lived with her Grandmother in a little house that hung right over the edge of the water. When you looked out of the window, there it was and you could drop things down into it.

Now this was about the funniest little house that ever was. It made you think of Santa Claus' house because there were so many things in it that you would like to ask questions about. But best of all, was a ship with real sails and ropes and a cabin—just like a ship. Hilda's father had made it for her and it would sail on the water.

"Let's see if it will," said Jimmy. So they climbed down on some rocks by the edge and Hilda put the little ship in the water. And she let Jimmy and the Scratch Cat hold the string and pull it about.

"Now let's pretend," said Jimmy, "that we are all going to sail away on this ship, and I'll be the captain and you and Hilda will live in the cabin."

"And where will we go?" asked the Scratch Cat.

"To Norway," said Hilda.

"What's at Norway?" asked Jimmy.

"Oh, snow and *snow* and icicles and reindeer and sleds —everything nice," said Hilda.

"Maybe that's where Santa Claus lives," said the Scratch Cat. And just then, instead of sailing away to Norway to find Santa Claus' house, they heard someone coming and looking around they saw the Funny Man who had been hunting them everywhere.

Of course he sat down on the rocks beside them so he could look at the little Norway ship.

"Hilda knows where Santa Claus lives," said the Scratch Cat.

"Well then," said the Funny Man, "maybe Hilda will tell us a Santa Claus story." But Hilda shook her head and looked embarrassed.

"You tell one," said Jimmy.

"Please, please do," said all the children together.

So the Funny Man did, and this is the story.

"Now when Santa Claus first decided to turn toy-maker and call Christmas Eve to leave nice things in girls' and boys' stockings, he was a young man with coal black hair. Of course that may seem very strange to you because all the pictures that you see nowadays have a snow white beard and hair. But I'll tell you about that. His hair turned in a night from coal black to snow white! And all from worry too.

"You see the first year that he made toys he didn't know the addresses of very many children, so of course he didn't make so very many. But when they were all finished, and as pretty as could be, he put them in his pack and looked around and scratched his head, saying:

"Now just how am I to get around with all this stuff!"

"Now Santa Claus had an old uncle who lived with him and earned his board doing chores. And as he was old and moved slowly he *sometimes* seemed stupid. But he wasn't —*far* from it. Santa Claus rather depended on him to help him out whenever he got into a pinch and the Uncle always did his best. He'd say 'Now why don't you do this,' or 'Why don't you do that?' You see he had *ideas*, which are such useful things to have, especially for people like Santa Claus who are always trying to turn out something new.

" 'How shall I manage this big toy pack?' said Santa Claus one day.

" 'Why not go on a big kite?' said the Uncle. 'We can easily make one in the work shop. Then I'll hold the string and you fly away in whichever direction there are children's chimneys.'

"Would you believe it, it worked like a charm, and Santa Claus flew from housetop to housetop, delivered all the toys and was back home before sun-up.

"But the next year Santa Claus said to his Uncle, 'This kite won't do *at all*.'

" 'Why not?' asked the Uncle.

" 'Well,' said Santa Claus. 'All of the children who got Christmas presents last year have told their friends about it, so this year *they'll* be hanging up their stockings too. I get letters every day, from just *everywhere*, asking me to call. So of course I must make many, *many* more toys that I ever did before. So what's to be done?'

" 'I have it,' said the Uncle, quick as a flash.

" 'What?' asked Santa Claus.

" 'That great big stork that lives on your roof all the year round, he could take you just as well as not,' said the Uncle.

" 'Why certainly,' said Santa Claus. 'I'll ask him.'

"But the stork said, 'Certainly *not!*' that he had quite enough to do taking babies where they belonged, that anyway they couldn't depend on him, for like as not on Christmas Eve he might be very busy. So that settled that.

"'Uncle, you'll have to think of something else,' said Santa Claus, who was beginning to get rather worried as Christmas was only a month away.

"So the Uncle thought and thought and finally said, 'We might go in a ship and sail around the edge of the world and stop wherever we saw a chimney and just take a chance that a child lived there.'

"'But that would take an awful lot of walking,' said Santa Claus.

"'I might go along and help,' said the Uncle.

"But that wouldn't have done at all for he had rheumatism and never could have kept up. However even though he moved slowly the poor old Uncle was good at ideas and said that he would keep right on thinking.

"And Santa Claus kept thinking too, but he was *such* a hand to worry and really began to get thin and a little bit cross. So the doctor looked severe and said that he must have fresh air and exercise and should take a daily walk in the woods.

"Now the first day that Santa Claus started on a health walk he met a pretty little reindeer, shaking and shivering and *so* thin that you could count its ribs. Of course kindhearted Santa Claus took it straight home, gave it his own supper and made a bed for it down beside the furnace in the cellar.

"The next day when he went for his second health walk in the woods exactly the same thing happened again. Funny wasn't it? So of course he took this second hungry little reindeer home, gave it his own supper and made a bed for it down beside the furnace in the cellar.

"Well if you'll believe it that same thing happened for eight different days, which meant eight reindeers down in Santa Claus' cellar.

"'I'm really about crazy,' said Santa Claus, two days

before Christmas. 'There are those eight reindeer getting fatter and fatter and what in the world am I to do with them? If I turn them out in the snow they'll never find anything to eat. They'd starve to death.'

" 'It won't do any good to worry,' said the wise Uncle.

" 'I can't help it,' said poor Santa Claus. 'Now just look at these hundreds and hundreds of toys to be delivered in one short night. Did *any* man *ever* have so much to worry him?'

"Then all of a sudden his coal black hair turned snow white. Just like that! It alarmed his Uncle so that he shuddered and shook until an idea popped into his head. The best one yet. It was a *wonderful* idea.

" 'I have it!' said the old man, dancing in circles, round and round the room. Santa Claus had to chase him to make him stop and tell what the idea was.

" 'What is it, Uncle, for goodness sake?' said Santa Claus, shaking him.

" 'Hitch the eight reindeer up to a sleigh full of toys and drive like the wind round the world in a single night,' said the Uncle, all out of breath.

" 'Why, of course!' said Santa Claus. 'Why didn't we think of it before?"

"So they set to work and built a fine shining black sleigh and made a beautiful red harness and hung dozens of jingle bells on it, then hitched up the eight giddy little reindeers who were now in fine trim—fat and sleek, and anxious to be off.

"So you see everything turned out nicely and the children's stockings were all filled and Santa Claus got back on Christmas morning before light, which pleased him very much as he does not like to be peeped at. You know that."

"Then what did he do?" asked the Scratch Cat.

"Nothing much, probably," said the Funny Man. "But just sit by the fire with his Uncle and talk about the folly of worrying about *anything*."

Now while this Santa Claus story was being told, they had all hunched up close together because the wind had changed and it was getting cold. Just talking about deep snow and reindeer makes you cold through. So they ran, holding hands, all the way home, just to get warmed up. Hilda told them goodbye at her house, where they could smell the supper that her Grandmother was cooking.

Now as the days went by each one was a little colder than the one before, and you heard this person say "Not long till the holidays" and the other person say "No, it will soon be *Christmas*." Then the stores began to have pretty sparkling things in the windows and the market was full of good things to eat—turkeys and cranberries and so on. And folks talked about secrets, *but didn't tell them*.

They were exciting days and you got up early in the morning and stayed up till the very last minute at night, then teased your mother to allow you to stay up just a little longer. There were so many things to talk about. There was that letter to be written to Santa Claus, and with the greatest care, so that he would bring exactly the right things. Then there was your Christmas piece to learn for Speaking Day. But first of all Jimmy and the Scratch Cat wanted to earn some Christmas Present money for, you see, they wanted to get something nice for *all* their friends. The Scratch Cat's mother said that she would give her a nickel for every hundred that she got in spelling. But Jimmy found another plan for earning money—he had to, because he almost *never* got a hundred in spelling.

"How would you like to help me color the Christmas pictures on the blackboard, Jimmy?" asked the Teacher.

Jimmy said that he would like it, so he made pictures of holly, and Stars of Bethlehem, and Santa Claus. They were very pretty and everybody liked them. So Jimmy went home and made lots of colored pencil pictures.

"Christmas pictures for sale for five cents," said Jimmy the next day to his Mother. So she bought the first one. Then the Boarding House Ladies each took one, and then what do you suppose? The Funny Man bought all the rest of the pictures! So Jimmy counted the money and found that he had all together, two quarters, three dimes and four nickels, which is supposed to be a dollar. Think of it—a dollar for Christmas present money.

When Jimmy told the Scratch Cat she said, "What shall I do? I'm not getting any hundreds." So she had to wipe dishes, but she worked hard and finally had a dollar, too.

Then the children went shopping and bought and bought till they had loads of bundles, which they hid under their beds because they were secrets.

"It's time to write letters to Santa Claus," said the Funny Man one day.

"Pen and ink letters?" asked Jimmy.

"Why not send him telegrams?" said the Funny Man. "Might scare the old fellow."

"Let's!" said the children.

So they went up to the Funny Man's room to talk.

"First," said the Funny Man, "Just what do you want him to bring you?"

"I want a Buffalo-Bill suit," said the Scratch Cat.

"That won't do," said the Funny Man. "You'll get Santa Claus all mixed up. He'll think you are a boy. Think of something else."

"All right then," said the Scratch Cat. "I'll take roller skates—a sled—some games—and lots of candy."

"Now Jimmy?" said the Funny Man.

"I'll take the same," said Jimmy.

So the Funny Man wrote a telegram and this was it:

Mr. S. Claus,
The North Pole,
Arctic Ocean.

Kindly deliver two sleds, two pairs roller skates, games and plenty of candy on December twenty-fifth to—

The Scratch Cat and Jimmy—
Care of The Funny Man.

"Will it get there for sure?" asked Jimmy.

"*Sure* as *sure*," said the Funny Man.

So after that was done they set to work to learn their Christmas Speaking Day pieces. It was funny that they had both picked on the same one — "The Night Before Christmas When All Through The House." The Teacher said that it was all right, and the Funny Man said that it was a *good thing* in case either of them should forget. And of course they were in dialogues and choruses with other boys and girls.

Hilda and the Scratch Cat were angels in white dresses and Jimmy wore a Father Time Suit and a white wig and a cotton beard. Lots of parents came and nobody forgot their pieces. Then the Teacher said "Merry Christmas to you all." And they said, "The same to you," which was the end of Speaking Day.

But the best of all was to be next day which *was* Christmas. The Funny Man was having a party at the boarding house. Yes, sir. Jimmy and his mother and Hilda and her Grandmother and Jeff and the Scratch Cat. So it was all arranged. The next morning was fine and snowy and everybody put on their best clothes.

When they got to the boarding house the doors and windows had wreaths and there stood the Funny Man himself—all fixed up and saying "Wish you a Merry Christmas!" before you could even open your mouth.

But when you got into the hall—goodness! There stood a big glistening Christmas Tree with real lights and balls and shiny things. And under it they saw two pairs of roller skates and two sleds, besides games and candy and some other things that Santa Claus had brought to the others. Then, when you were just beginning to believe that it was really *you* standing there, out jumped a big tall Santa Claus all in red with a cap and beard. Then he took a telegram out of his pocket and read it out loud, and it was the very one that Jimmy and the Scratch Cat had sent to Santa Claus. And right under the tree were the things which they had *asked for*. Which shows that if you are particular you'll get the things you want. And Hilda got a doll off the tree, and mittens and candy. There was something for everybody. After that Jimmy and the Scratch Cat gave *their* nice presents all around.

Then the Funny Man said, "Let's all give three cheers for Santa Claus." Which everybody did. And Santa took off his cap and bowed, and that made his beard fall off. Well, whom do you suppose it was? Jeff! And there were a lot of presents for him too like the others.

Soon after that the Boarding House Ladies said that everything was ready. So they all went out to the dining room, two and two together. It was lit with beautiful red candles and trimmed with holly and there was a huge turkey and rows and rows of other dishes all filled with good things. And the last thing was a big plum pudding with smoke going up and it looked exactly like a picture.

After that the Funny Man and Jeff took all the children and the new sleds and they went coasting down past the Church. It was *wonderful*, but finally they got so cold that they had to go in and the rest of the day all the folks at the Funny Man's Christmas party sat around the fire and ate nuts and candy and played with the new games.